Prickly Ballroom

by Ian Smith and Sean Julian

FRANKLIN WATTS
LONDON·SYDNEY

First published in 2011 by
Franklin Watts
338 Euston Road
London
NW1 3BH

Franklin Watts Australia
Level 17/207 Kent Street
Sydney
NSW 2000

A CIP catalogue record for this book is available
from the British Library.

ISBN 978 0 7496 9469 2 (hbk)
ISBN 978 0 7496 9475 3 (pbk)

Series Editor: Jackie Hamley
Series Advisor: Catherine Glavina
Series Designer: Peter Scoulding

Printed in China

Franklin Watts is a divison of
Hachette Children's Books,
an Hachette UK company.
www.hachette.co.uk

One morning, Porcupine saw a poster for a dance competition.

Porcupine loved
to dance.

He just needed a partner.

But all the animals said,
"Sorry, Porcupine, you're
too prickly!"

Porcupine was sad.
He wondered what
he could do.

He tried putting on
a thick coat ...

... but his prickles
poked through.

He tried putting corks
on his prickles ...

... but the corks fell off.

Porcupine went to see
Rabbit, the hairdresser.

14

"No one will dance with me because I'm so prickly. Please cut off my prickles!" he told Rabbit.

Rabbit had a better idea.
"Meet me at the dance
tonight!" she said.

When Porcupine arrived,
all the other animals
were already there.

He was very nervous.

But then Rabbit arrived.
On her paws she wore a
pair of thick oven gloves.

"Brilliant!" laughed
Porcupine.

Porcupine and Rabbit
started to dance.

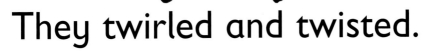

They twirled and twisted.

23

They jumped and jived.

They spun and shook.

The Judges gave them first prize.

Porcupine was delighted.
"Thank you, Rabbit!"
he cheered.

Then the animals danced
together all night long ...
with Porcupine!

Puzzle 1

Put these pictures in the correct order.
Now tell the story in your own words.
How short can you make the story?

furious   caring

kind

shy   naughty

nervous

Choose the words which best describe each character. Can you think of any more? Pretend to be one of the characters!

Answers

Puzzle 1

The correct order is:

1e, 2c, 3b, 4f, 5a, 6d

Puzzle 2

Rabbit The correct words are caring, kind.

The incorrect word is furious.

Porcupine The correct words are nervous, shy.

The incorrect word is naughty.

Look out for more Leapfrog stories:

The Little Star
ISBN 978 0 7496 3833 7

Mary and the Fairy
ISBN 978 0 7496 9142 4

Jack's Party
ISBN 978 0 7496 4389 8

Pippa and Poppa
ISBN 978 0 7496 9140 0

The Bossy Cockerel
ISBN 978 0 7496 9141 7

The Best Snowman
ISBN 978 0 7496 9143 1

Big Bad Blob
ISBN 978 0 7496 7092 4*
ISBN 978 0 7496 7796 1

Cara's Breakfast
ISBN 978 0 7496 7797 8

Croc's Tooth
ISBN 978 0 7496 7799 2

The Magic Word
ISBN 978 0 7496 7800 5

Tim's Tent
ISBN 978 0 7496 7801 2

Why Not?
ISBN 978 0 7496 7798 5

Sticky Vickie
ISBN 978 0 7496 7986 6

Handyman Doug
ISBN 978 0 7496 7987 3

Billy and the Wizard
ISBN 978 0 7496 7985 9

Sam's Spots
ISBN 978 0 7496 7984 2

Bill's Baggy Trousers
ISBN 978 0 7496 3829 0

Bill's Bouncy Shoes
ISBN 978 0 7496 7990 3

Bill's Scary Backpack
ISBN 978 0 7496 9458 6*
ISBN 978 0 7496 9468 5

Little Joe's Big Race
ISBN 978 0 7496 3832 0

Little Joe's Balloon Race
ISBN 978 0 7496 7989 7

Little Joe's Boat Race
ISBN 978 0 7496 9457 9*
ISBN 978 0 7496 9467 8

Felix on the Move
ISBN 978 0 7496 4387 4

Felix and the Kitten
ISBN 978 0 7496 7988 0

Felix Takes the Blame
ISBN 978 0 7496 9456 2*
ISBN 978 0 7496 9466 1

The Cheeky Monkey
ISBN 978 0 7496 3830 6

Cheeky Monkey on Holiday
ISBN 978 0 7496 7991 0

Cheeky Monkey's Treasure Hunt
ISBN 978 0 7496 9455 5*
ISBN 978 0 7496 9465 4

For details of all our titles go to: www.franklinwatts.co.uk

*hardback